DC
SUPER-
PETS!™

Published by Stone Arch Books, an imprint of Capstone
1710 Roe Crest Drive, North Mankato, Minnesota 56003
capstonepub.com

Library of Congress Cataloging-in-Publication Data
Names: Korté, Steven, author. | Baltazar, Art, illustrator. | Norris, Paul (Paul Leroy), 1914–2007, creator.
Title: Storm! : the origin of Aquaman's seahorse / by Steve Korté ; illustrated by Art Baltazar.
Other titles: DC Super-Pets! Origin stories.
Description: North Mankato, Minnesota : Stone Arch Books, an imprint of Capstone, [2022] | Series:
DC super-pets origin stories | "Aquaman created by Paul Norris." | Audience: Ages 6–8. | Audience:
Grades K–1. | Summary: Aquaman is holding a contest to choose a successor for his retiring seahorse,
Swifty, but the contest is interrupted by the appearance of an evil ice dragon—and when Storm
jumps in to help and saves Aquaman, the choice is clear: Storm is Aquaman's new seahorse.
Identifiers: LCCN 2021023536 (print) | LCCN 2021023537 (ebook) | ISBN 9781663959126 (hardcover)
| ISBN 9781666328868 (paperback) | ISBN 9781666328844 (pdf)
Subjects: LCSH: Aquaman (Fictitious character)—Juvenile fiction. | Sea horses—Juvenile fiction. |
Dragons—Juvenile fiction. | Superheroes—Juvenile fiction. | Contests—Juvenile fiction. |
CYAC: Superheroes—Fiction. | Sea horses—Fiction. | Dragons—Fiction. |
Contests—Fiction. | LCGFT: Superhero fiction.
Classification: LCC PZ7.K8385 Ss 2022 (print) | LCC PZ7.K8385 (ebook) | DDC 813.54 [Fic]—dc23
LC record available at https://lccn.loc.gov/2021023536
LC ebook record available at https://lccn.loc.gov/2021023537

Designed by Hilary Wacholz

STORM!

The Origin of Aquaman's Seahorse

by **Steve Korté**
illustrated by **Art Baltazar**
Aquaman created by **Paul Norris**

STONE ARCH BOOKS
a capstone imprint

EVERY SUPER HERO NEEDS A
SUPER-PET!

Even Aquaman!
In this origin story, discover
how Storm the seahorse
became the Sea King's
loyal steed . . .

Deep beneath the surface of the ocean, a party is taking place in the underwater city of **Atlantis**.

King Arthur, who is also known as the mighty **Super Hero Aquaman**, is the ruler of Atlantis. He has gathered his loyal subjects together for a special occasion.

It is a party in honor of Swifty the seahorse. Swifty is retiring after serving as Aquaman's royal steed for many years.

All of Aquaman's loyal subjects
are **celebrating**!

Topo the octopus is playing many musical instruments at once. Ark the seal is juggling oysters. Tusky the walrus and Porpy the porpoise are having a fin-wrestling contest. Geoffrey the hammerhead shark is cracking open hard-shelled snacks with his head.

Aquaman holds up his hand for quiet.

"Today, we'll hold a contest to choose the seahorse who will serve as my next steed," he says. "**The contest will test speed, strength, and bravery.** The first event is a race to the shore and back."

A dozen oysters line up on the ocean floor to make a starting line for the race.

Four seahorses approach the line. Their names are Storm, Zoom, Coral, and Spiny.

"**Ready . . . set . . . ,**" Aquaman calls.

Aquaman raises his trident up high.

Then he slams it down.

The four seahorses charge forward.

Coral reaches the shore first. She is in the lead as the seahorses turn back.

As they all speed toward Atlantis, Storm pulls ahead.

Aquaman watches the seahorses near the finish line. He announces, **"And the winner is . . . Storm!"**

The seahorses have only a moment to rest before the strength contest is scheduled to begin.

Suddenly, a huge school of fish swim through Atlantis in a great hurry. The fish look very frightened.

Aquaman is able to speak with any type of sea life using only his mind.

"What's wrong?" he asks the fish. "Where are you going?"

The fish don't stop to answer, but Aquaman hears some of them reply with "**monster**" and "**great danger**."

Aquaman immediately starts swimming toward the danger. He is joined by Tusky, his loyal walrus friend.

Storm watches for a moment. Then he decides he wants to help if he can. He follows Aquaman and Tusky.

As they swim away from Atlantis, Aquaman notices that the water is getting colder.

"That's odd," he says. "These are usually very warm waters."

Suddenly, a giant blue ice dragon swims into view!

The dragon opens its mouth and hurls a blast of icy breath. Aquaman and Storm swim out of the way, **but Tusky is not fast enough**.

The dragon's freezing breath traps the walrus within a solid block of ice.

Aquaman quickly rubs his hands together.

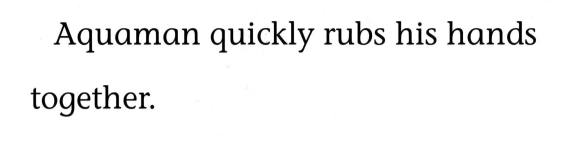

"This will slow down the dragon!" he says to Storm.

The movement of Aquaman's hands creates swirling balls of water that he can use as weapons.

Aquaman throws the balls of water at the dragon.

ROAR!

The dragon lets loose another blast of freezing breath. The balls of water turn into balls of ice.

PLUNK! PLUNK! PLUNK!

The chunks of ice drop to the ocean floor before they can hit the dragon.

An evil smile stretches across the sea monster's face.

Aquaman swims toward the dragon. His hand is closed into a strong fist.

"It's time to knock you out cold!" he says.

Aquaman draws back his arm, ready to deliver a powerful blow.

Just then, the monster opens its mouth wide.

The dragon blasts the hero with its freezing breath. Aquaman is instantly frozen inside a thick block of ice.

"Aquaman and Tusky are trapped," Storm says. **"It's up to me now!"**

Storm charges forward and crashes his head against the dragon.

BLAM!

The monster is thrown off-balance.
But it quickly recovers and shoots a
blast of ice at Storm.

Storm darts away from the attack.

"Using my head didn't work," says Storm. **"So I'll try using my tail!"**

Storm zooms forward. Before the dragon can react, Storm wraps his powerful tail around the monster's neck. The dragon is unable to blast Storm with its icy breath.

Storm holds on tight and throws the monster to the ocean floor.

The ice dragon is knocked out cold.

"Now to use my mind to call for help," says Storm. **"Calling all swordfish! Calling all swordfish!"**

A school of swordfish is swimming nearby. They hear Storm's call for help and swim over to join him.

"Aquaman and Tusky are trapped," says Storm. **"Can you rescue them?"**

The swordfish quickly go to work. They use their razor-sharp bills to crack open the ice around Aquaman and Tusky.

Within seconds, the pair are freed!

Aquaman looks up and sees two beluga whales swimming above him. He uses his mind to speak to them.

"I need your help," he says. "Can you move this dragon into a cave?"

The beluga whales are happy to help their king. They carry the sleeping monster into a nearby cave.

But Aquaman knows this solution will only last a short time. **The ice dragon will soon wake up.**

Storm swims up to the mouth of the cave and looks inside. The dragon is slowly opening its eyes.

"I have an idea!" says Storm.

The seahorse starts spinning his body like a top. He spins at a fantastic speed!

Storm's spinning creates a whirlpool of water. The whirlpool grows **larger and larger**. It forms a giant wall of water in front of the cave.

Just then, the dragon wakes up!

ROAR!

The monster blasts the spinning wall of water with its freezing breath.

The dragon's breath freezes the wall of water.

The monster is completely sealed inside the cave behind a solid chunk of ice.

"Nice work, Storm!" says Aquaman. "That ought to hold the dragon for now. Later, we'll move it to arctic waters far away from Atlantis."

Back at Atlantis, Aquaman has an announcement for his subjects.

"Congratulations, Storm," he says. **"You are the new Royal Steed of Atlantis!** Not only were you the fastest swimmer, but you showed great strength and bravery during the ice dragon battle!"

Storm glows with pride. "Hop on, sire!"

Aquaman leaps onto Storm's back. The seahorse kicks his tail hard, and the pair speed through the water.

"With you at my side," Aquaman says to Storm, **"I know my underwater kingdom will be safe!"**

STORM!

REAL NAME:
Storm

SPECIES:
Seahorse

BIRTHPLACE:
Atlantis

HEIGHT:
8 feet

WEIGHT:
240 pounds

Super Hero Owner:
AQUAMAN

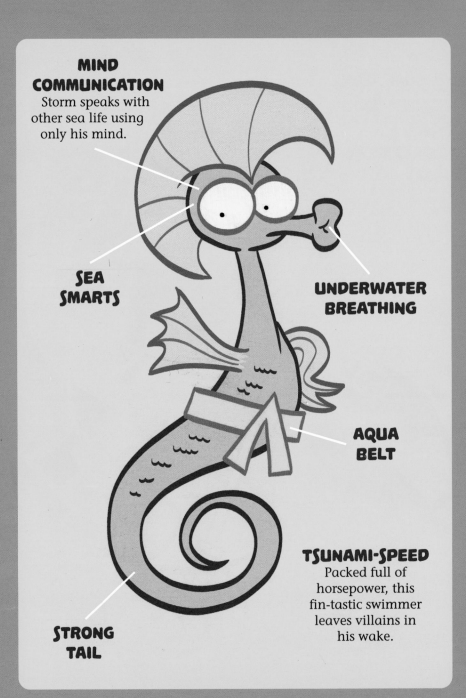

MIND COMMUNICATION
Storm speaks with other sea life using only his mind.

SEA SMARTS

UNDERWATER BREATHING

AQUA BELT

STRONG TAIL

TSUNAMI-SPEED
Packed full of horsepower, this fin-tastic swimmer leaves villains in his wake.

HERO PET PALS!

GEOFFREY

Super Hero Owner:
MERA

TUSKY

Super Hero Owner:
AQUALAD

VILLAIN PET FOES!

**MISTY AND
SNEEZERS**

Super-Villain Owner:
BLACK MANTA

FRANKIE

Super-Villain Owner:
OCEAN MASTER

STORM JOKES!

How did the octopus make Aquaman laugh?
With ten-tickles!

What does Aquaman do when he sees a blue whale?
He tries to cheer it up!

Why did the seahorse cross the ocean?
To get to the other tide!

GLOSSARY!

announcement (uh-NOWNS-muhnt)—official information that is said out loud

arctic (ARK-tik)—having to do with the North Pole or the area around it

porpoise (POR-puhss)—an ocean mammal, related to a dolphin, with a rounded head and short, blunt snout

retire (rih-TIRE)—to leave a career and stop working

solution (suh-LOO-shuhn)—the answer to a problem

steed (STEED)—an animal used or trained for riding

subject (SUHB-jikt)—someone who lives in a kingdom and is ruled by a king or queen

trident (TRY-dent)—a long spear with three sharp points at its end

whirlpool (WURL-pool)—water that moves very quickly in a circle

READ THEM ALL!

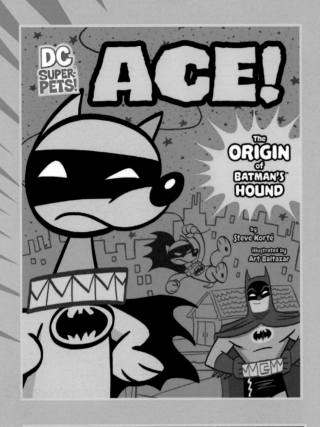

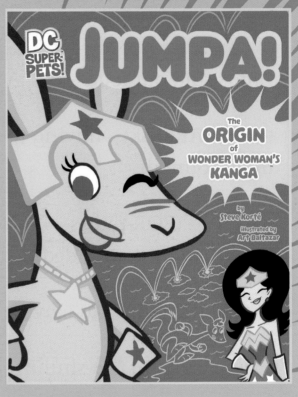

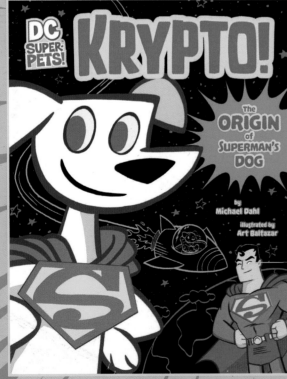

ONLY FROM capstone

DC SUPER-PETS!
B'DG!
The ORIGIN of GREEN LANTERN'S ALIEN PAL

by Steve Korté
illustrated by Art Baltazar

DC SUPER-PETS!
BEPPO!
The ORIGIN of SUPERMAN'S MONKEY

by Steve Korté
illustrated by Art Baltazar

DC SUPER-PETS!
COMET!
The ORIGIN of SUPERGIRL'S HORSE

by Steve Korté
illustrated by Art Baltazar

DC SUPER-PETS!
STORM!
The ORIGIN of AQUAMAN'S SEAHORSE

by Steve Korté
illustrated by Art Baltazar

AUTHOR!

Steve Korté is the author of many books for children and young adults. He worked at DC Comics for many years, editing more than 600 books about Superman, Batman, Wonder Woman, and the other heroes and villains in the DC Universe. He lives in New York City with his husband, Bill, and their super-cat, Duke.

ILLUSTRATOR!

Famous cartoonist **Art Baltazar** is the creative force behind *The New York Times* best-selling, Eisner Award-winning DC Comics' Tiny Titans; co-writer for Billy Batson and the Magic of Shazam!, Young Justice, Green Lantern: The Animated Series (comic); and artist/co-writer for the awesome Tiny Titans/Little Archie crossover, Superman Family Adventures, Super Powers!, and Itty Bitty Hellboy. Art is one of the founders of Aw Yeah Comics comic shop and the ongoing comic series. Aw yeah, living the dream! He stays home and draws comics and never has to leave the house! He lives with his lovely wife, Rose, sons Sonny and Gordon, and daughter, Audrey! AW YEAH, MAN! Visit him at www.artbaltazar.com.